Birthday F

MW01253621

Written By:

Kim Mitzo Thompson
Karen Mitzo Hilderbrand

Illustrated By:

Steve Ruttner

Cover Illustration By:

Sandy Haight

Musical Scores By:

Hal Wright

Twin 432 – Birthday Party Songs

(Tape/Book Set) –ISBN# 1-57583-051-5
(CD/Book Set) – ISBN# 1-57583-364-6

Twin Sisters Productions, Inc. • (800) 248-TWIN • www.twinsisters.com

Table of Contents

Birthday Party Song Lyrics

Cooperation Games

Games For Rainy Days

The NEW Happy Birthday Song

Click your fingers with me and sing along,
    because we're going to learn the new birthday song.
Clap your hands with me and sing along,
    because we're going to learn the new birthday song.

Happy birthday to you, to you.
    Today's your special day.
Happy birthday to you, to you.
    Everyone shout "Hooray!"
Happy birthday to you, to you.
    Today's your special day.
Happy birthday to you, to you.
    Everyone shout "Hooray!"

March around the table, and sing along,
    because we're going to learn the new birthday song.
Stomp around the table, and sing along,
    because we're going to learn the new birthday song.
(chorus)
Click your fingers with me and sing along,
    because we're going to learn the new birthday song.

Birthday Bee Bop

Everyone come dance with me.
Everyone, let's shout and sing.
That's the birthday bee bop.
That's the birthday bee bop.

Now hop three times, and then turn around.
Put your right foot out, and let's all touch the ground.
Hey, hop to the music. Yeah!
That's the birthday bee bop.

(chorus)
Okay, swing your hips, and let's all turn around.
Put your left foot out,
    and now touch the ground.
Let's hop to the music. Yeah, that's great!
That's the birthday bee bop.

Bee bop, bop, bop.
Bee bop, bop, bop.
Bee bop, bop, bop.
Bee bop, bop, bop.
Bee bop, bop, bop.
We're doin' the birthday bee bop!
Wave to a friend.
Turn around, both feet out,
and touch the ground.
Now hop to the music.
That's the birthday bee bop.

(chorus)

TWIN 432 - Birthday Party Songs

Pin The Bow On The Birthday Bear

Pin the bow on the birthday bear.
Pin the bow and see...
 is it in the right place right under his chin?
Or is it down close to his knee?
Pin the bow on the birthday bear.
You know where it should be.
Is it crooked or straight?
Is it in the right place, or did you place it on his teeth?

The birthday bear, the birthday bear,
 let's pin the bow on the birthday bear.
The birthday bear, the birthday bear,
 let's pin the bow on the birthday bear.

Let's turn you around three times,
 with the blindfold on your eyes.
With the bow in hand, you must walk real slow,
 for on the bear that bow must go.
Pin the bow on the birthday bear.
 Please don't look or peek.
Is it up or down?
Are you turned around,
 or did you place it on his cheek?
Pin the bow on the birthday bear.
 Are you dizzy from the spin?
Is it in the right place? It's looking close.
It's under the birthday bear's chin.

(chorus)

 TWIN 432 - Birthday Party Songs

The Hokey Pokey

You put your right foot in,
 you put your right foot out;
 you put your right foot in,
 and you shake it all about.
You do the hokey pokey,
 and you turn yourself around.
That's what it's all about!

You put your left foot in,
 you put your left foot out;
 you put your left foot in,
 and you shake it all about.
You do the hokey pokey,
 and you turn yourself around.
That's what it's all about!

3. You put your right hand in, etc.
4. You put your left hand in, etc.
5. You put your right shoulder in, etc.
6. You put your left shoulder in, etc.
7. You put your right hip in, etc.
8. You put your left hip in, etc.
9. You put your backside in, etc.
10. You put your whole self in, etc.

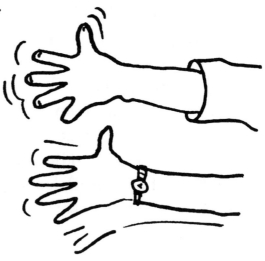

You do the hokey pokey.
You do the hokey pokey.
You do the hokey pokey.
That's what it's all about!

TWIN 432 - Birthday Party Songs

Let's Do The Hokey Pokey

TWIN 432 - Birthday Party Songs

Pass The Hot Potato

C'mon everyone, form a circle, and sit down. We're going to play "Pass The Hot Potato." Here's how you play: When the music starts, I want you to pass the potato around the circle. Remember, pretend that the potato is hot, and pass it quickly. But, when you hear Bessie the cow (Moooo), the person caught holding the potato must leave the circle. Are you ready? Start passing!

(Music)

*(Moooo) Oh, no, I hear Bessie the cow. Who has the potato?
Okay, give the potato to the friend sitting next to you and move out of the circle. Don't worry...we'll play again soon. Let's go, and start passing!*

(Music)

(Moooo) Okay, who has the potato this time? You need to move out of the circle too. Ready? Let's start passing!

(Music)

(Moooo) I hear Bessie the cow again. Remember, pass the potato quickly. Okay if you had the potato you need to move away from the circle too. Are you ready everyone? Let's go!

(Music)

*(Moooo) There's Bessie the cow. The circle's getting smaller. Everyone move close together.
It will be easier to pass the potato. Ready? Start passing.*

(Music)

(Moooo) We have some great potato passers here. Keep passing!

(Music)
(Moooo) There's Bessie! There are only a few people left. Everyone move close together. Ready? Go!

(Music)
(Moooo) This is fun. One more time!

(Music)
(Moooo) Congratulations! I think we have a winner! Moooo!

Let's Play Musical Chairs

Let's play musical chairs. Gather 'round everyone. Do you know how to play musical chairs? It's easy, you march around the chairs when you hear the music playing, and when the music stops, like this, you find the nearest chair and sit down. Unfortunately, there are not enough chairs for everyone. So, if you are left without a chair, then you will have to stand back until the game is over. Each time the music stops and everyone sits down, a chair will be taken away. The last person left in the game is the winner. Now before we start, I do need to remind you that if you push a friend to sit down in a chair, you will have to leave the game. Okay everyone, let's start marching!

(Music)

Quick! Find a chair and sit down! Good job! Okay, if you don't have a chair, move to the side please. Let's remember to take one chair away. And.....march!

(Music)

Remember to sit down! Great! Now if you don't have a chair, move to the side, please. Ready? Go!

(Music)

Are you having fun? Fantastic! Remember to take one chair away. Get up and....march!

(Music)

It keeps getting harder, doesn't it? Now, let's listen to the next song and all walk slowly, like an elephant.

(Music)

Raise your hand if you're still in the game. Okay, let's walk!

(Music)

Wow! We sure have some great-looking elephants at this party! Let's take another walk.

TWIN 432 - Birthday Party Songs

(Music)

Okay, let's pull another chair away. It's getting exciting, isn't it? Are you ready to hop around the chairs like a bunny? Well, start hopping!

(Music)

It's hard to hop for that long. You must have been practicing. Let's do it again.

(Music)

Everyone's looking pretty tired. How many are left? C'mon. Get up and hop, hop, hop!

(Music)

Okay, we're done hopping. To finish the game, let's put on our marching shoes again.

(Music)

Quick! Find a chair and sit down! Okay, take another chair away.
Up..and march!

(Music)

There are some expert marchers in this group. Lift your legs....and march!

(Music)

One more time, and we'll have a winner. If you are left after this round, then you are definitely a winner at musical chairs! Let's go!

(Music)

Alright, we have a winner! Come over and get a prize!

TWIN 432 - Birthday Party Songs

Birthday Limbo

Gather around for the Birthday Limbo,
    under the limbo stick we'll go.
Bend your back, don't touch the stick now,
    carefully, bend back real low.

It's the Birthday Limbo,
    you have to wait your turn.
It's the Birthday Limbo,
    this game you'll quickly learn.
It's the Birthday Limbo,
    the stick is moved and then,
It's the Birthday Limbo,
    now lower you must bend.

(chorus)
It's the Birthday Limbo,
    it's lower to the ground.

It's the Birthday Limbo,
    and harder I have found.
It's the Birthday Limbo,
    who will win today?
It's the Birthday Limbo,
    you've won the limbo game!

(chorus)
Whoa, whoa, whoa! (chorus)
Whoa, whoa, whoa! (chorus)

TWIN 432 - Birthday Party Songs

Let's Do The Limbo

You Will Need:

Music boom box to play the "Birthday Limbo" song
A limbo stick (a mop or broom handle will work just fine)

Directions:

Explain to the children that the limbo is a type of dance that originated in the West Indies. (You may want to show the location on a globe.) The dancers bend at the knees and lean backward as they move underneath a bar or limbo stick. The limbo stick is moved lower and lower making the dance more difficult. The dancers may not touch the ground or the limbo stick with their hands while bending underneath the stick.

Have two volunteers hold the limbo stick, starting at shoulder height, and have the children practice bending under the stick. Once the music starts, have the children lower the stick after each child has taken a turn. An adult should stand nearby to spot or help each of the children as they go underneath the limbo stick.

It's Your Special Day Parade

Do you hear the trumpet fanfare?
They are playing just for you.
Do you hear the drums 'a beating?
Everyone's marching to this tune.
Up and at'em, stand real tall.
Start marching while we sing.
It's your birthday and you know
  what joy this day will bring.

It's Your Special Day Parade,
  with friends and family here to say,
"It's Your Special Day Parade,
  we are thankful for your birthday."

Do you hear the big bass tubas?
Listen to the flutes' sweet sound.
The trombones are marching past,
  and there is music all around.
The clarinets are quite off-tune,
  but at least they're having fun.
The bells are ringing out,
  but my favorite sounds are drums.

(chorus)

Do you hear the trumpet fanfare?
They are playing just for you.
Do you hear the drums 'a beating?
Everyone's marching to this tune.
Up and at'em, stand real tall.
Start marching while we sing.
It's your birthday and you know
  what joy this day will bring.

(chorus 2x)

TWIN 432 - Birthday Party Songs

Simon Says

Simon says, Simon says,
    do only what Simon says.
Listen carefully while we
    play the "Simon Says" game.

Do you know how to play Simon Says? It's easy. Listen to each direction like: "Simon says put your hands on your head." or "Simon says 'jump up and down'," and follow Simon's directions. But if you hear a direction that Simon doesn't say, like "touch your elbow," or "wave to a friend," then don't do it, because Simon didn't say to. Are you ready to play? You can do it!

Simon says, turn around.
Simon says, touch the ground.
Simon says, reach for the sky.
Now wave goodbye.
Oh, Simon didn't say to!

Simon says, jump up and down.
Simon says, march all around.
Simon says, pat your head.
Now rub your tummy instead.
Don't do it! Simon didn't say to!
(chorus)

Simon says to walk real slow.
Simon says, touch your toes.
Simon says, make a funny face.
Now run in one place.
Oh, Simon didn't say to!

Simon says clap your hands real loud.
Simon says, make an "oinking" sound.
Simon says, touch your thumbs.
Now pretend to play the drums.
I caught you! Simon didn't say!
(chorus)

       TWIN 432 - Birthday Party Songs

Okay, it's time to make this game a little tougher. I'm going to be Simon and give you directions. Remember, if I don't say "Simon says" before my direction, don't do it! Ready? Set? Go!

Simon says, put your hands in the air.
Simon says, pat your head.
Simon says, turn around.
Simon says, touch the ground.
Rub your belly.

I caught you! You shouldn't rub your belly, because I didn't say "Simon says 'rub your belly'." You're doing a great job. C'mon, here we go!

Simon says, march in place.
Simon says, swing your arms.
Stop! No, don't stop. I didn't say Simon says!

Simon says, touch your shoulders.
Simon says, touch your waist.
Simon says, touch your knees.
Touch your toes!
I caught you!

Simon says, run in place.
Simon says, hop like a bunny.
Simon says, stop!
Great job! Let's sing!
(chorus 2x)

Duck, Duck, Goose

Duck, duck, duck, duck, duck, duck, duck, goose!
Run around the circle as fast as you can,
    after you gently tap a friend's head.
Run around the circle, that's how the game goes,
    so someone else can be the "Goose" instead!

Who will be the next one picked?
No one knows for sure.
To be the "goose" is lots of fun.
I hope it will be my turn.

"Duck, Duck Goose" is a funny name,
    but I really do like this game.
I want to run because I'm real fast,
    but I'll wait until I'm picked at last.

(chorus)
Who will be the next one picked?
We'll have to wait and see.
It's fun to listen for that sound,
    "Goose!" They're running around.

Faster, faster, you must go,
it's like running a race.
Faster, faster, to the spot, and then
    sit down in the right place.

(chorus)

Ten Layer Birthday Cake

Since today is your birthday
I think I will make, a delicious ten layer birthday cake.
How will I bake it you ask with a grin.
I'll need ten pounds of flour before I begin.

Four dozen eggs from my Uncle Jack's farm,
   and three bags of sugar, now don't be alarmed.
Butter, yes butter, I'll need 22 sticks,
   or 24, let me check my arithmetic.

Since today is your birthday
I think I will make, a delicious ten layer birthday cake.
Since today is your birthday
I think I will make, a delicious ten layer birthday cake.

The first will be chocolate, with sprinkles galore.
With caramel and fudge on two, three and four.
Five, six and seven, may I suggest,
   bananas and marshmallows are simply the best.
Eight, nine and ten, now I'm almost through.
I'll add strawberries and a cherry or two.

(chorus)

Out of the oven, it smells so divine.
I told you my cake would turn out just fine.
Now onto the table, no wait, wait, wait, stop!
My cake's on the floor. It just fell with a "plop".

(chorus)

    TWIN 432 - Birthday Party Songs

Hop To The Finish Line

Children of all ages will enjoy this traditional potato sack race!

You Will Need: Burlap Sacks

Using burlap fabric, make your own potato sacks by sewing the sides to create a sack. Make sure to make the sacks the appropriate size for the age group of children expected at the party. King-size pillow cases would work for young children.

Directions:

Because you will need plenty of room, outdoors is the best place for this game to be played. Ask the children if they like to run races. Then, ask the children if they would like to participate in a race in which they would not be able to run, but would have to hop! Pass out the potato sacks and have each child step into a sack, holding the ends around their chest. Once children are familiar with hopping in the sacks to move forward, introduce the race. Have children line up horizontally on a designated "start" spot. Have a finish line clearly marked ahead. (Make the distance appropriate to the children's age. If the distance is too far away, they may become frustrated.) Give a verbal direction of:

Ready! Set! GO!

The first child to cross the finish line is the winner!

Cooperation Games

Teaching children how to work together cooperatively can be a challenge. The cooperation games listed below encourage children to work with a partner or group to accomplish a certain goal in a fun way.

Keep The Balloon In The Air

Divide the children into two separate groups. Give each group a balloon. Tell the children that the object of this game is for each group to work together to keep the balloon in the air. Toss the balloons in the air and have each group swat their balloon to keep it moving. Children will soon learn that gentle swats and controlled movements will make them more successful. The group that keeps their balloons in the air the longest is the winner.

The "Don't Drop The Beach Ball" Game

Have children work in pairs for this fun game. Using a soft blown-up beach ball, tell children that the object of this game is NOT to drop the beach ball. The only rule is that they cannot touch the beach ball with their hands. Partners must stand facing each other while the beach ball is placed between their stomachs. The partners must press gently together to hold the beach ball in place. Children will learn by experience that if the ball is squeezed too tightly, it will pop out. Have children line up horizontally at a starting point. Tell them that they are to walk with their partner to the finish line while they squeeze the beach ball. The first pair to cross over the finish line with the beach ball still in place is the winner! If a pair drops the beach ball, then they must run back to the starting point and begin again.

©Twin Sisters Productions, Inc.

The Bean Bag Toss

Cut empty gallon milk containers in half. Put tape around the perimeter edge in case it is sharp. Have children face a partner, standing 3-4 feet away. Give each child a milk container. Place a bean bag in one of the partner's milk containers. The partner must swing the milk container to throw the bean bag to the other partner. This partner must try to catch the bean bag in his/her container. After each successful toss, have the partners move back one step. The pair that is the farthest apart without dropping the bean bag on the ground is the winner!

The "Find Your Shoes" Game

Divide the children into two teams. Have all of the children take off their shoes. Mix up the shoes and place them in one huge pile. Have the children form two lines. When you say "GO" have the first child from each line run to the pile of shoes. The two children must find their own shoes and put them on. When they have their shoes on, tell them to run back to their team and tap the hand of the next person in line. That person should run to the pile of shoes and put on their own shoes as well. The game continues until one of the teams has all of their shoes on. Children will want to play this game over and over!

Make Your Own Birthday Hats

Directions:

Use the pattern on the next page to make your own birthday party hats!
Make a photocopy of the pattern for each child, or trace the pattern on
another sheet of white paper. To make a sturdy pattern, trace the
pattern on a piece of tag board. Have the children decorate their
birthday crowns with stickers, stars, glitter and markers. Cut a piece of
12" x 18" construction paper in half horizontally. Tape or staple the ends
together to fit each child's head. Glue the decorated birthday crown on
the front of the hat as shown below. This is a fun activity to do at a
birthday party before the cake is cut!

TWIN 432 - Birthday Party Songs

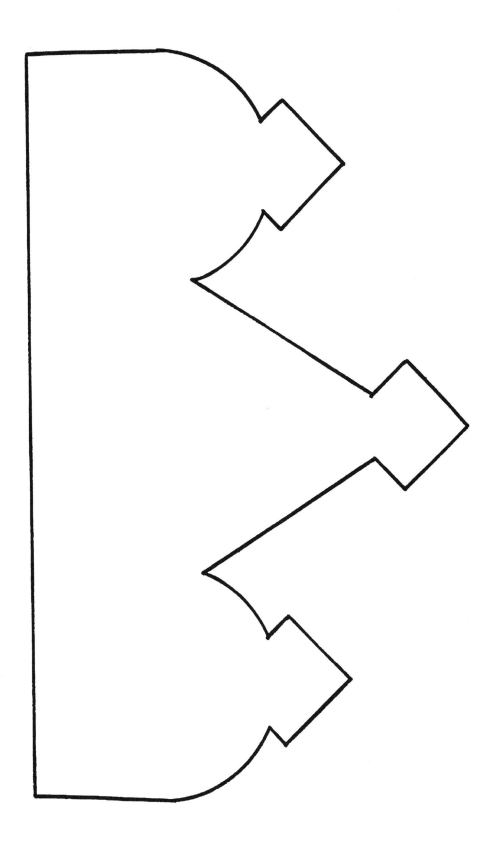

TWIN 432 - Birthday Party Songs

Games For Rainy Days

Four Corners

This is a great game to play in a basement. Number each corner of a room or basement with the numbers 1 through 4. One person should stand in the center of the room with his/her eyes closed tight. The person should count aloud to 20. All of the children should be instructed to walk quickly and quietly to one of the four corners. The children must be at a corner when the counter says "20" or they will be out of the game. Then the counter shouts out a corner. If the person says "Corner Number 2," then all of the children standing in corner number 2 will have to sit down in the middle of the room. The counter then counts to 20 again while the remaining children move to another corner. The game continues until one person is left!

Doggie, Doggie, Where's Your Bone?

Place one chair in front of the room. Have a group of children sit behind the chair a few feet away. Have one child sit in the chair, his/her back toward the group, with a plastic bone, or some other small object underneath the chair. Choose one child to go and fetch the bone by pointing to him/her quietly. That child should return to his/her seat as quietly as possible and place the bone behind his/her back. All of the children then should place their hands behind their backs and pretend that they have the bone. Then the group of children should say, "Doggie, Doggie, where's your bone? Somebody took it from your home. Guess who?" The person then turns around and tries to guess who has the bone. If the person is not found after three guesses, that person with the bone becomes the Doggie. If the Doggie guesses correctly, then he/she is the Doggie for a second turn.

©Twin Sisters Productions, Inc.